DAVY
and the
GOBLIN

I dedicate this edition
of DAVY AND THE GOBLIN
to my son Gregory,
with love.

Greg Hildebrandt

DAVY and the GOBLIN

Story by Charles E. Carryl
Illustrated by
GREG HILDEBRANDT

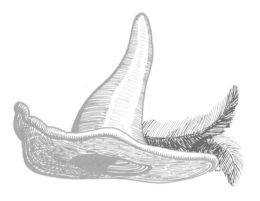

The Unicorn Publishing House
New Jersey

Designed by Jean L. Scrocco
Edited by Heidi K. L. Corso, Michael Wendt, and Rita Wendt
Printed in Singapore by Singapore National Printers Ltd. through Palace Press,
San Francisco, CA
Reproduction Photography by the Color Wheel, New York, NY

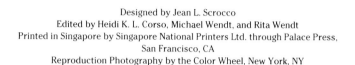

♦ ♦ ♦ ♦ ♦

Distributed in Canada by Doubleday Canada, Ltd., Toronto ON

♦ ♦ ♦ ♦ ♦

Printing History 15 14 13 12 11 10 9 8 7 6 5 4 3 2 1

♦ ♦ ♦ ♦ ♦

Library of Congress Cataloging-in-Publication Data is available.
Library of Congress Catalog Card Number: 88-32641

More Colorful Classics
In This
Easy-to-Read
Little Unicorn Classic Series

PETER PAN
ANTIQUE FAIRY TALES
PINOCCHIO
THE WIZARD OF OZ
HEIDI
A CHRISTMAS CAROL
POLLYANNA
TWENTY THOUSAND LEAGUES

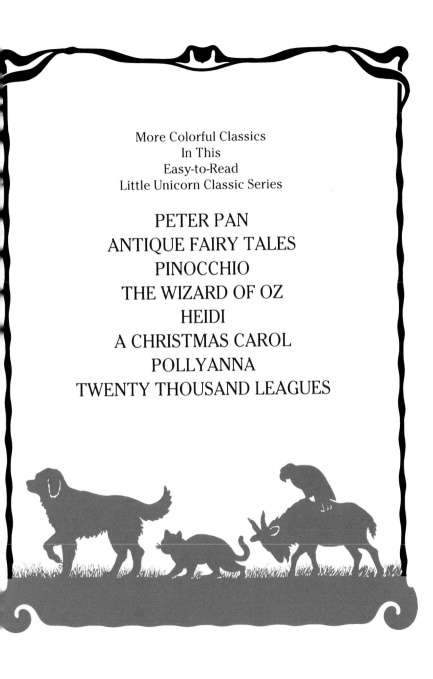

CAST OF CHARACTERS

Rob McCann – Davy
Betty McGuire – Mother Hubbard
Joseph D. Scrocco, Jr. – Badorful, the Giant
Gregory Hildebrandt, Jr. – Robin Hood
Greg Hildebrandt – Sham-Sham
Larry Weiss – Sindbad
Gene O'Brien – The Coachman
William McGuire – Robinson Crusoe
Dr. Edward Lowell – Thimbletoes, Prime Minister to the Queen
Jean L. Scrocco – Her Gossamer Majesty, the Fairy Queen
John Vazaios – Berrylegs
Heidi Corso – Fairy in Waiting to the Queen
Thomas Roberts – Member of the Fairy Court
Phyllis Foley – Davy's Grandmother
Sunday's Dinner – Gobobbles, the Turkey

And introducing
The Goblin
as
The Goblin

LIST OF ILLUSTRATIONS

DAVY
and the
GOBLIN

It happened one Christmas Eve, when Davy was about eight years old. That particular Christmas Eve was a snowy one. Davy had come to spend Christmas with his dear old grandmother.

In the city where Davy lived, the storm played all manner of tricks. It swooped down upon old gentlemen and blew their hats out of sight. As for the old ladies, the icy wind twisted their dresses around their ankles. It blew snow in their faces. Here people stayed indoors, close to great blazing wood fires. Outside the storm howled and roared. It covered roads and houses.

Davy had been out with his sled trying to have a little fun with the weather; but this storm wasn't friendly to little boys. He went back into the house.

Davy wandered around the house looking for something to do. He slid down the banisters and teased the cat.

At last, as evening was coming on. Davy curled himself up in the big easy chair facing the fire. He began to read once more about the marvelous things that happened to little Alice in Wonderland. He could smell dinner cooking downstairs, and he was just daydreaming about his favorite food when he suddenly discovered a little man smiling at him with all his might.

This little man was a very unusual person indeed. He was only about a foot high, but his head was as big as a coconut, and he had great, bulging eyes. He was all dressed in red.

Now, there's no use in saying that Davy was not frightened. He saw that the little man was carefully picking the hottest embers out of the fire and eating them happily. Davy watched to see if the little man would burst into flames; but he finished his coals in safety. Then he nodded cheerfully at Davy and said:

"I know you. You are the little boy who doesn't believe in anything the storybooks tell you. Now, all that is very foolish and wrong. I'm a goblin myself and I've come to take you on a Believing Voyage."

At this the Goblin skipped across the room to the big clock. He rapped sharply on the front of the case with his knuckles. To Davy's surprise, the great thing fell over on its face upon the floor as softly as if it had been a feather bed. Davy now saw that the clock was really a sort of boat, with a wide seat at each end. The Goblin climbed in and sat down.

For a moment Davy had a wild idea of calling for help, but after a moment he climbed into the clock and took his seat. The clock rose from the floor and made a great

swoop towards the window. "I'll steer," shouted the Goblin! "You look out for cats and dogs!"

The first thought that came into Davy's mind when he found himself outdoors was that it had stopped snowing and that the air was quite still and warm. The moon was shining brightly. The house suddenly disappeared.

This was such a surprise that Davy was quite worried. He wondered what had happened to his grandmother. Before he had time to ask, he saw his grandmother floating through the air on her rocking chair. She was quietly knitting, and the chair was rocking gently as she went by. Next came Mrs. Frump, the cook, who was carrying her pots and kettles. Then came the maid. She was sitting on a ladder with a pile of coals for the fire in her lap. Solomon, the housecat, was nowhere to be seen.

Davy looked down. Below him, in the top of a tree, two sparrows lay sleeping in their nest. Davy saw that they were using one of his mittens for a blanket. I am sorry to say that Davy knew where the other mitten was and was ashamed to say anything about it.

All at once the clock began rolling over in the air. He had just time to grasp the sides of it, to keep himself from falling out.

"Don't be afraid!" cried the Goblin. As he said this, the clock stopped rocking and sailed smoothly away. Davy now noticed that the Goblin was glowing with a bright, rosy light.

"That's the coals he had for his supper," thought Davy. "I think he must be as warm as a piece of toast." The little boy was laughing softly to himself. The Goblin, who had been staring at the sky, suddenly ducked his

head, and cried "Storm!" The next moment the air was filled with cats falling from the sky. They were of all sizes and colors. At least a dozen of them fell sprawling into the clock. Among them was Solomon, his grandmother's cat, with one of Davy's mittens drawn over his head. Davy had put it there earlier to tease the poor cat.

Now, Davy would never have teased Solomon if he had had any idea that cats could talk. Solomon cried out excitedly, "Cry! I should think I had enough to cry about today! I've had bits of cloth tied to my tail and I've had some milk with pepper in it. And now I have this nightcap on!"

All this was certainly enough to cry about; but what else Solomon had to complain of will never be known. Just at this moment, an old tabby cat screamed out, "Barkers!" All the cats sprang over the side of the clock, and disappeared.

"But it was such fun you know," said Davy, feeling guilty.

"Fun for *you*,"said the Goblin. "Here come the Barkers!" he added. As he said this, a shower of little blue woolly balls came tumbling into the clock. They immediately began scrambling about in all directions and yelping loudly. The Goblin pulled a large magnifying glass out of his hat and began examining these strange visitors.

"Bless me!" cried the Goblin, turning very pale, "they're sky-terriers. We must get away from these fellows quickly. Here, jump into my hat."

Davy did just that. As they sailed away in the hat, the clock quietly rolled over once and then drifted away.

Davy was surprised to find that the hat was so large,

but it was very unpleasant to travel in. It spun around like a top, until Davy began to feel dizzy.

"I had no idea your hat was so big," Davy said to the Goblin.

"I can make it any size I please," said the Goblin. Suddenly, he fell out of the hat. He instantly disappeared from sight.

Davy peered over the edge of the brim, but the Goblin was nowhere to be seen. The little boy found himself quite alone.

Strange-looking birds now began to fly around him. Then, a great creature with rumpled feathers landed upon the brim of the hat. It said "I'm a Cockalorum," and flew away. Looking down at his legs, Davy discovered that the crown of the Goblin's hat had entirely disappeared. That left nothing but the brim, upon which he was sitting. Then he found the hat was really nothing but an enormous ball of wool, which was rapidly unwinding. He suddenly found himself falling through the air.

He was on the point of screaming when he discovered that he was falling very slowly. The next moment he struck something hard, which gave way with a sound like breaking glass. He fell crashing into the branches of a large tree.

The tree into which Davy had fallen was so comfortable that he lay back between two branches and enjoyed the rocking. Davy lazily wondered what had become of the Goblin, and whether this was the end of the Believing Voyage. Then he sat up on the branch in great surprise, for he saw that the tree was loaded with plums. Winter had disappeared very suddenly, and he saw that he had

fallen into a place where it was broad daylight. He carefully selected the largest and most tasty-looking plum he could find. Looking up he saw the Cockalorum, perched upon the bough beside him. "Perhaps it's a sugar plum," he said, and then flew away.

"Perhaps it is!" exclaimed Davy; taking a great bite of the plum. To his surprise he found his mouth full of very bad tasting soap. At the same moment the white leaves of the plum tree suddenly turned over and showed the words "APRIL FOOL" printed on their under sides. Davy scrambled down from the tree to the ground.

He found himself in a large garden, with walks winding among other plum trees in every direction. Walking along one of these paths, he suddenly saw a small figure standing nearby.

He was as flat and thick as a pancake. Also, Davy could see through him as clearly as though he had been made of glass. Actually he was made of lemon candy. He was neatly dressed, with a funny hat and had a large book under his arm. This curious-looking creature was standing before a high wall. His back was to Davy, and he was watching a large hole in the wall about a foot from the ground. Davy, walking up close behind the candy man, said very politely, "I dropped in here —"

Before he could finish the sentence the Hole-keeper said snappishly, "Well, drop out again — quick!"

"I fell down ever so far," said Davy, beginning his story over again, "and at last I broke through something —"

"That was the barley sugar skylight!" yelled the Hole-keeper. "And I shall certainly be boiled! Now see here.

This must be a secret between us."

Davy promised and the Hole-keeper picked up his book and said, "Well, just wait till I can't find your name." He began quickly turning over the pages.

Davy saw to his surprise, that there was nothing whatever in the book.

"How do you expect to find my name in *that* book? There's nothing in it."

"Ah! that's just it, you see," said the Hole-keeper, smugly; "I look in it for the names that ought to be out of it. Oh! here you aren't! Your name is Rupsy Frimbles."

With that Davy felt himself gently lifted off his feet and pushed headfirst into the hole. When he came out at the further end, he found himself in a large room. The floor was so slippery that Davy could hardly stand. Against the walls on all sides were long rows of little tin chairs.

The only person in the room was a little man, who looked something like the Hole-keeper, but denser and darker. After a startled look at Davy, he disappeared through a door at the further end of the room. The next moment a lot of creatures just like him came into the room. At this moment a voice called out, "Bring Frungles this way." The crowd gathered around him and began to push him across the room.

"That's not my name!" cried Davy.

Davy caught sight of the Hole-keeper, also struggling in the crowd. His great book was hugged tightly to his chest.

We are going to be taken before the king," said the Hole-keeper, in a high voice. The next moment they were dragged up to a low platform. The king was sitting there

on a gorgeous tin throne. He was just like the rest of the creatures, but he was a little larger. He wore a blue paper coat and a sparkling tin crown. In his hand was a long white wand, with red lines running around it like a barber's pole. He called out, "Are the chairs buttered? Yes? Then sit down!"

The crowd sat down. The king frowned at the Hole-keeper. "Who broke the barley-sugar skylight?" he asked. Getting no answer, the king pointed at the Hole-keeper with his wand and roared: "Boil *him*, in any case!"

"Don't you go with them!" shouted Davy. "They're nothing but a lot of sticky candy!"

At this the king gave a frightful scream. He aimed a furious blow at Davy with his wand. Then everything was wrapped in darkness. Davy felt himself being whirled along, head over heels through the air. All at once he found himself running rapidly down a long street with the Goblin at his side.

"What were they?" asked Davy, all out of breath.

"Butterscotchmen," said the Goblin, who had turned blue. "You see, they always butter their chairs so that they won't stick fast when they sit down."

"Are they coming after us now?" asked Davy.

"Of course they are," said the Goblin. "We must keep running until we get to the Amuserum. It's like a museum. By the way, how much money have you? We have to pay to get in."

Davy began to feel in his pockets. He found to his surprise, that they were all filled with a lot of rubbish. First he pulled out a hard-boiled egg, without the shell, stuck full of small tacks. Then came two slices of toast.

Then came a little glass jar, filled with large flies. Then came a tart filled with little stones, two chicken bones, a bird's nest and many other odd things. At last he found a piece of money.

The street suddenly came to an end at a brick wall. There was a small round hole in the wall, with the words "PAY HERE" printed above it. The Goblin whispered to Davy to hand in the money through this hole. The next moment the wall rose slowly before them like a curtain. He and the Goblin were left standing in a large square.

A figure came hurrying through the square. He was carrying a sign on a pole that read:

JUST RECEIVED! THE GREAT FRUNGLES THING!
ON EXHIBITION IN THE PLUM-GARDEN!

At the sight of these words the mob began streaming out of the square after the pole bearer.

The Goblin said "Let's look at the curiosities."

Davy followed and found, sorry to say, that the curiosities were the things that had been in his pockets a few minutes before. They were placed on little tables. The Goblin had taken a telescope out of his pocket and was examining the objects with the closest attention. As he did this, he was muttering to himself, "Wonderful!" as if he had never seen anything like them before.

The Goblin then turned his telescope towards Davy. Davy, peering closely through the large end, saw him suddenly shrink to the size of a small beetle, and then disappear altogether. Davy reached out with his hands to grab the telescope and found himself staring through a round glass window into a farm yard, where a red Cow stood looking up at him.

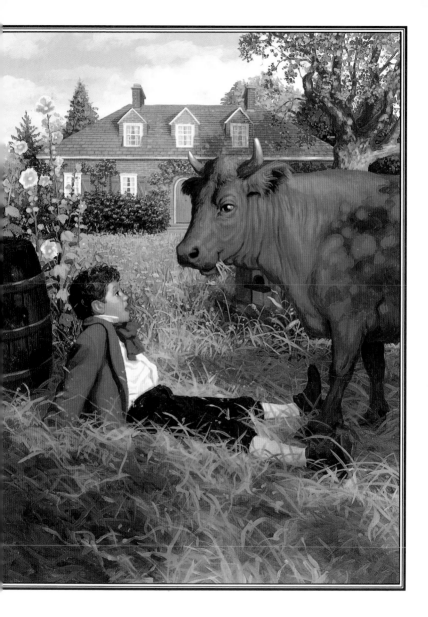

It was quite an ordinary-looking Cow, but she stared so earnestly up at Davy that he felt certain she had something to say to him. Just at this moment the window suddenly flew open, and he fell upon a pile of hay in the farmyard. The Cow stood looking at him with a very serious expression. Presently the Cow said in a sad voice, "The old gray goose is dead, so we've buried her in the garden. We thought gooseberries would come up, but they didn't. Nothing came up but feathers."

"What else is there in the garden?" asked Davy.

"Nothing but the bean-stalk," said the Cow. "You've heard of 'Jack and the Bean-stalk,' haven't you?"

"Oh! yes, indeed!" said Davy, "I should like to see the bean-stalk."

"You cant *see* the beans talk," said the Cow, gravely. "You might *hear* them talk. By the way, that's the house that Jack built. Mother Hubbard lives there."

"I'd really love to see Mother Hubbard," said Davy.

"Well," said the Cow, "if you'll look in at the kitchen window you'll probably find her playing the piano and singing a song."

Just as the Cow had said, Mother Hubbard was there, sitting at the piano and just starting to sing. The piano was very remarkable. The top of it had shelves, on which stood all the kitchen dishes. In the under part of it, at one end, was an oven with glass doors, through which he could see several pies baking. She sang in a high and quivering voice.

While she was singing the song, little handfuls of tiny stones were being thrown at her through one of the kitchen windows. By the time the song was finished her

lap was quite full of it.

"Who's throwing the gravel?" asked Davy.

"It's Gobobbles," said the Cow, calmly. "You'll find him around at the front of the house."

"Boy," said Mother Hubbard, looking through her spectacles, "you shouldn't throw gravel."

"I didn't," said Davy, "it was Gobobbles!"

"So I supposed," said Mother Hubbard. "It would have been far better if he had been cooked last Christmas instead of stuffing him and then letting him go. You'll find *him* in front of the house."

Davy went carefully around the corner of the house. Gobobbles proved to be a large turkey with all his feathers taken off. He was tied fast in a baby's high chair and was thumping his chest with his wings. As Gobobbles caught sight of him he said sulkily:

"I can't stand boys. They're so everlastingly hungry. Now don't deny that you're fond of turkey."

"Well, I *do* like turkey," said Davy.

"Of course you do!" said Gobobbles, tossing his head. "I suppose Christmas is coming, of course. It's *always* coming!" said Gobobbles angrily.

"I don't mind having it come," said Davy.

"Oh, don't you, indeed!" said Gobobbles. "Well, then I don't mind having *you* go!" Here he began hopping his chair forward in such a threatening manner that Davy turned and ran away.

As he went around the corner of the house again he found himself in a pleasant lane. Looking back, he saw to his dismay, that Gobobbles had in some way got loose from his high chair. He was coming after him, thumping

himself in a perfect frenzy. Davy did not wait for a second look but started off at the top of his speed.

Gobobbles, however, was a fast runner and came closer and closer until he seemed to be just at Davy's heels. At this instant something sprang upon his back; but before he could cry out, a head was suddenly thrust over his shoulder. He found the Goblin, who was now a bright purple color, staring him in the face and laughing with all his might.

"You needn't be afraid of Gobobbles!" said the Goblin. "He's busy enough just taking care of himself. You see, he's wanted for Christmas."

Just at this moment a loud, rumbling noise, followed by a tremendous sneeze, shook the ground.

"What's that?" whispered Davy to the Goblin.

"It's only Badorful," said the Goblin, laughing. "He's always snoring and waking himself up. I suppose it's sleeping on the ground that makes him sneeze. Let's have a look at him."

Davy was alarmed at seeing a giant, at least twenty feet high, sitting cross-legged on the ground. On the grass beside him lay a huge club with iron knobs. Creeping vines were curling themselves among these knobs, as though the club had been lying there untouched for a long time.

The giant was talking to himself in a low tone, and the Goblin said laughing: "He's making poetry!"

Badorful looked up with a feeble smile and merely said, "Just listen to this:"

My age is three hundred and seventy-two,

And I think, with the deepest regret,
How I used to pick up and voraciously chew
The dear little boys whom I met.
I've eaten them raw, in their holiday suits;
I've eaten them curried with rice;
I've eaten them baked, in their jackets and boots,
And found them exceedingly nice.
But now that my jaws are too weak for such fare,
I think it exceedingly rude
To do such a thing, when I'm quite aware,
Little boys do not like to be chewed.
And so I contentedly live upon eels,
And try to do nothing amiss,
And I pass all the time I can spare from my meals
In innocent slumber — like this.

Here Badorful rolled over upon his side and was instantly fast asleep.

At this moment a farmer, with bright red hair called out, "Here comes Gobobbles!" Davy and the Goblin watched Gobobbles go by like a flash. A crowd of people armed with pitchforks followed right behind. Gobobbles bounded over the hedges and stone walls like a kangaroo, waving his wings. Davy and the Goblin now hurried off to catch Gobobbles. Presently they came upon the crowd of farmers who were dancing around a large white object lying on the ground. Davy expected to see Gobobbles; but the white object proved to be the Cockalorum.

"I thought we were chasing Gobobbles!"

"Of course you did," said the Goblin; "but things often turn out to be different from what you expect."

With this the Goblin disappeared. The Cockalorum and the dancing farmers had also disappeared, and he found that he was quite alone in a dense wood.

"I wish things wouldn't change about so!" Davy said.

Presently the trees and bushes directly before him moved silently apart and showed a broad path. Turning quickly around a large tree, Davy suddenly came upon a little butcher's shop. There was a sign on the shop reading, "ROBIN HOOD: VENISON." Robin himself, wearing a clean white apron over his suit of green, stood in the doorway. As he caught sight of Davy he said, "Steaks? Chops?" quite like an everyday butcher.

"No, not today, thank you," said Davy.

"Tomorrow?" inquired Robin Hood.

"No, I thank you," said Davy again.

"Will you want any yesterday?" asked Robin Hood.

"I think not," said Davy, beginning to laugh.

"Then what did you come here for?" said Robin Hood.

"Well, you see," said Davy, "I didn't know you were this sort of person at all. I always thought you were an archer, like William Tell."

"He wasn't an archer," said Robin Hood. "He was a crossbow man, the crossest one that ever lived."

Davy walked on, hoping the forest would soon come to an end, until the path came to a little brick shop. It had a green door and a sign which read:

SHAM-SHAM: BARGAINS IN WATCHES.

"Well," said Davy, in amazement. "Of all places to sell watches." After a moment, he went up and knocked timidly at the door. There was no answer and Davy pushed open the door and went in.

The place was so dark that at first he could see nothing. Soon he discovered an old man with dark skin, mixing watches in a large iron pot.

"How many watches do you want?" he asked.

Davy said, "I don't want any watches today."

"Drat," said the old man, angrily beating the watches with his spoon; "I'll never get rid of them!" "You're a pretty spectacle! I'm another. What does that make?"

"A pair of spectacles, I suppose," said Davy.

"Right!" said the old man. And pulling an enormous pair of spectacles out of his boot he put them on and began reading aloud from a piece of paper:

> My recollectest thoughts are those
> Which I remember yet;
> And bearing on, as you'd suppose,
> The things I don't forget.
> But my resemblest thoughts are less
> Alike than they should be;
> A state of things, as you'll confess,
> You very seldom see.
> And yet the mostest thought I love
> Is what no one believes—
> That I'm the sole survivor of
> The famous Forty Thieves!

At this moment a big commotion began among the watches. There was no doubt about it, the pot was boiling. Sham-Sham, cried out, "Don't tell me a watched pot never boils!" He sprang to his feet and, pulling a pair of pistols from his belt, began firing at the watches. Davy

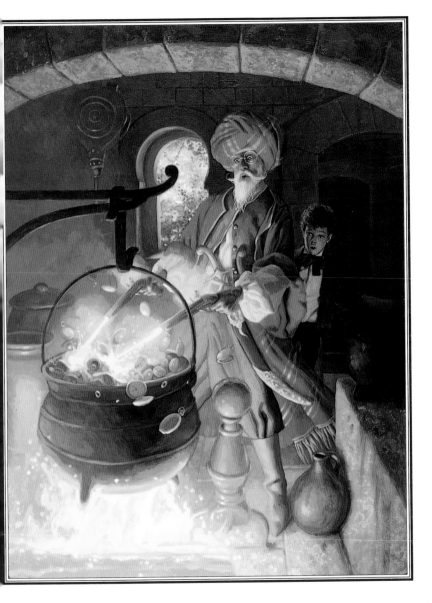

who had had quite enough of Sham-Sham by this time, ran out of the door.

To his great surprise he found himself in a sort of underground passage. It was lighted by grated openings overhead. Walking along, Davy noticed that he was now in a sort of tunnel made of fine grass, like the inside of a bird's nest. The next moment he came out into an open space in the forest. To Davy's amazement, the Cockalorum was sitting upright in an armchair, with his head wrapped up in flannel.

The place was lit by a large chandelier that hung from the branches of a tree. Davy saw that a number of odd-looking birds were roosting on it. As Davy made his appearance the birds all cried out together, "Here's the doctor!" Before Davy could reply, the Hole-keeper suddenly appeared and said, "*He* isn't a doctor. His name is Gloopitch." At these words there arose a long, wailing cry; the lights disappeared, and Davy found himself on a broad path in the forest. The Hole-keeper was walking quietly beside him.

"By the way, you're not the postman, are you?"

"Of course I'm not," said Davy.

"I'm glad of that," said the Hole-keeper. "Would you mind delivering a letter for me?"

"Oh, no," answered Davy. It certainly was a large letter. Davy was much pleased to see that it was addressed:

Captain Robinson Crusoe,

Jeran Feranderperandamam, B.G.

"What does B.G. stand for?" said Davy.

"Baldergong's Geography, of course," said the Hole-keeper crossly. He turned into a side path, and disap-

peared in the wood.

As Davy walked along he found himself in the oddest-looking little country place. The little lawn was made of soft fur instead of grass, and here and there about the lawn little footstools were growing out of the fur. The trees were large feather-dusters. On a little mound at the back of the lawn stood a small house, built entirely of big conch-shells.

A creature in a blue coat and pink striped trousers was sitting, reading a little red book. Davy saw, to his surprise, that it was really the Goblin.

"Oh! you dear, old Goblin!" cried Davy, happy at again finding his friend.

"I do wish you wouldn't keep disappearing," said Davy.

"Rubbish!" said the Goblin. "That's only my way of getting a vacation."

"And where do you go?" asked Davy. Without answering, the Goblin began to fade away. If Davy had not grabbed his arm, the Goblin would have disappeared again. "Oh, I beg your pardon!" cried Davy, who was alarmed by the Goblin going away. "I don't really care about that. I only want to know what place this is," Davy said.

The Goblin stared about him for a moment. Then he said "Sindbad the Sailor's House. And here he comes now!"

Davy looked around and saw an old man coming toward them. He was dressed in a Turkish costume and wore a large turban and slippers. His white beard was so long that at every fourth step he trod upon it and fell flat

on his face. He took a seat upon one of the little footstools. Taking off his turban, he began stirring about in it with a large wooden spoon. As he took off his turban Davy saw that his bald head was neatly laid out in black and white squares like a chessboard. Davy looked into the hat and saw that it was filled with broken chess pieces.

"It's much better to play this way, isn't it?" asked Sindbad with a smile.

"It is?" said Davy, looking puzzled. "I think it looks much easier."

"Well, it isn't," said Sindbad. "There are more moves in my chess games than in twenty ordinary chess games." He stirred the chess pieces again and put the turban back on his head. "Check!" he called.

"This here Turk is the most reckless old story teller that ever was born," said the Goblin. "You can't believe half he tells you."

"I'd like to hear one of his stories," said Davy.

"All right!" said the Goblin. I know he'll give us a whopper!"

Davy looked at the Goblin curiously. "You know, he said, I believe that you've grown."

"Only to fit the clothes," said the Goblin. "If they had been too small I would have shrunk. It's much easier to find clothes that way."

As Davy and the Goblin sat down beside Sindbad, the sailor scowled at Davy. "It's no use talking to him," he said to the Goblin. "He's deaf as a post. But I'll tell you a story. I'll give you a sailor's story," Sindbad said.

Here he rose for a moment, hitched up his big trousers like a sailor and began:

A capital ship for a ocean trip
Was "The Walloping Window-blind;"
No gale that blew dismayed her crew
Or troubled the captain's mind.
The man at the wheel was taught to feel
Contempt for the wildest blow,
And it often appeared, when the weather had cleared,
That he'd been in his bunk below.
The boatswain's mate was very sedate,
Yet fond of amusement, too;
And he played hopscotch with the starboard watch,
While the captain tickled the crew.
And the gunner we had was apparently mad,
For he sat on the after-rail,
And fired salutes with the captain's boots,
In the teeth of the booming gale.
The captain sat in a commodore's hat,
And dined, in a royal way,
On toasted pigs and pickles and figs
And gummery bread, each day.
But the cook was Dutch, and behaved as such;
For the food that he gave the crew
Was a number of tons of hot-cross buns
Chopped up with sugar and glue.
And we all felt ill as mariners will,
On a diet that's cheap and rude;
And we shivered and shook as we dipped the cook
In a tub of his gluesome food.
Then nautical pride was laid aside,
And we cast the vessel ashore,

On the Gulliby Isles, where the Poohpooh smiles,
And the Anaganzanders roar.
Composed of sand was that favored land,
And trimmed with cinnamon straws;
And pink and blue was the pleasing hue
Of the Tickletoeteaser's claws.
On rubagub bark, from dawn to dark,
We fed, till we all had grown
Uncommonly shrunk when a Chinese junk
Came by from the torridy zone.
She was stubby and square., but we didn't much care,
And we cheerily put to sea;
And we left the crew of the junk to chew
The bark of the rubagub tree.

After the story, they set out for Sindbad's House. They all stepped in at the door, but as they did so, Sindbad and the Goblin vanished. Davy, instead of being inside the house, found himself standing in a dusty road, quite alone.

As Davy stood in the road, a huge bird came by. She was a large bird nearly six feet tall, and was carrying a covered basket and a door key hung around her neck.

"You don't happen to have a beefsteak about you," she asked. "No? Then hold my basket, I must go back."

"What's in it?" said Davy, taking the basket.

"Lay-overs for meddlers" said the big bird, who walked away and was soon out of sight.

"I think I'll take a peep," said Davy. He carefully raised the cover a little way and tried to look in. The next instant, the cover flew off the basket. Out poured a swarm

of little brown creatures, like snuff-boxes with legs. Davy made a frantic grab at one of them, but it instantly turned over on its back and blew a puff of smoke into his face. He rolled over in the road, choking. When he sat up again, the empty basket was lying on its side and not a lay-over was to be seen. At that moment the huge bird came in sight. Davy clapped the cover on the basket, took to his heels and ran for dear life.

The road was very dusty. It seemed to have no end, and it twisted and turned in a wild way. Davy ran on, afraid that the giant bird would catch up with him. It was lucky that Davy was a good runner. He felt that he could run for a week and not get tired. Certainly his legs felt very strong. Indeed, Davy would have run on for several more hours if he had not suddenly seen something ahead. He looked carefully and slowed down.

He soon came upon a horse and cab. The horse was fast asleep when Davy dashed against him. He woke up with a start, and, after whistling once or twice, went to sleep again. Davy noticed the word "RIBSY" painted in whitewash on his side in large letters. He was looking at this and wondering if it were the horse's name, when the door of the cab flew open and a man fell out. He was dressed in a clown's suit, with a field-marshal's hat. He held a whip in his hand. After a big yawn he looked up at Davy, and said, "Where to?"

"To B.G.," said Davy, remembering the Hole-keeper's letter.

When Davy stepped inside the cab he found the only seats were some three-legged stools huddled together. All the rest of the space was taken up by a large bath tub that

ran across the front end. Davy put his head out at the window. He saw that the cabman had climbed up on top of the cab and was throwing stones at the horse, which was still sleeping peacefully.

"Oh! don't do that," said Davy, anxiously. "I'd rather get out and walk." And with that Davy jumped out and began to walk.

"This is a very sloppy road," said Davy to himself. The dust had disappeared, and the sloppiness soon changed to so much wetness that Davy found himself in water up to his ankles. He saw, to his alarm, that the land in every direction seemed to be miles away. The depth of the water increased so rapidly that he soon found himself drifting out to sea. He felt much better when a boat came in sight sailing toward him. As it came near, it proved to be the clock, with a sail hoisted, and the Goblin sitting in the stern.

After climbing in, Davy looked over his shoulder and found that they were rapidly coming close to a little wooden dock. Beyond it stretched a sandy beach.

The clock struck against the timbers with a very large thump. Davy was thrown out, head over heels. The clock was turned completely around by the shock and was rapidly drifting out to sea again. The Goblin looked back sadly and said, "I don't know how to turn around!" The clock soon disappeared.

The beach was covered in every direction with little hills of sand. Before he had time to wonder about them, Davy caught sight of a man walking along the edge of the water. As the man drew nearer, Davy saw that he was dressed in a suit of brown leather, and that a dog, a cat,

and a goat were following at his heels, while a parrot was perched upon his shoulder.

Davy was certain that the man was Robinson Crusoe. He carried a very large gun. When it was fired, it only gave a faint squeak, and the bullet dropped quietly upon the sand. Robinson always seemed to be greatly surprised at this result. He looked long and anxiously down into the barrel of the gun. This was all so ridiculous that Davy had great difficulty in not laughing as he walked up to Robinson and handed him the Hole-keeper's letter. Robinson looked at him suspiciously as he took it.

Robinson took a long time to read the wet letter. Sometimes he would scowl horribly, then, again, he would chuckle to himself. Davy could not help seeing that it was simply a blank sheet of paper. When he finished reading the letter, Robinson stooped down and buried it.

"Can you shoot with *that* gun?" said Davy.

"Shoot! Why, it's a splendid gun!" said Robinson, gazing at it proudly. "I made it myself — out of a spyglass."

"But I don't see what you can shoot with it," said Davy.

Robinson suddenly turned pale. Quickly reaching out for his gun, he sprang to his feet.

Davy looked out to sea and saw that the clock and Goblin had come in sight again. They were heading directly for the shore with tremendous speed. The poor Goblin, who had turned sea-green, was wildly waving his hands to and fro. Robinson, who seemed to have run out of tooth-powder, was quickly loading his gun with sand. The clock struck the beach with great force, and turning completely

over on the sand, buried the Goblin beneath it. The clock began striking loudly, and the animals ran away in all directions.

Davy rushed up to the clock. To his great disappointment the Goblin had again disappeared. There was a smooth, round hole running down into the sand, as though he had gone directly through the beach.

"I suppose that's what they call going into the interior of the country," a voice said. Davy saw the Hole-keeper sitting on a little mound in the sand.

The little man must have been having a hard time since Davy had seen him. His complexion had quite lost its beautiful transparency. He was, however, more pompous than ever.

Presently the Hole-keeper stopped short and said, faintly, "It strikes me the sun is very hot here. In fact, I'm going back into the raw material. See here, Frinkles," he continued, beginning to speak very thickly; "wrap me up in my shirt and mark the packish distin gly. Take off shir quigly!" Davy just had time to pull the poor creature's shirt over his head and spread it quickly on the beach, when the Hole-keeper fell down and melted away into a compact lump of brown sugar.

Davy was very moved by this sad incident. In fact, he was so disturbed that he was on the point of going away without marking the package. Suddenly, he caught sight of the Cockalorum standing close beside him, holding an inkstand with a pen in it in one of his claws.

"Oh! thank you very much," said Davy, taking the pen. "Will you please tell me his name?"

"Mark him '*Confectionery*,' " the Cockalorum replied.

Davy, after a last look at the package of brown sugar, turned away. He was setting off along the beach again, when he heard a gurgling sound coming from behind a sand dune. He was startled at seeing an enormous whale lying stretched out on the sand basking in the sun. The creature had on a huge white garment, buttoned up in front, with a lot of live seals flopping and wriggling at one of the button holes. It had a great chain cable leading from them to a pocket at one side. Before Davy could leave, the Whale called out, "How d'ye do, Bub?"

"I'm pretty well, I thank you," said Davy. "How are you, sir?"

"Hearty!" thundered the Whale, "but it's rather warm lying here in the sun."

"What do whales eat?" he asked, thinking it was a good time for picking up a little information.

"I'm particularly fond of small buoys."

"I don't think that's very nice," said Davy.

"Oh! don't be frightened," bellowed the Whale, good-naturedly. "I don't mean live boys. I mean the little red things that float about in the water."

"Is it nice being a Whale?" said Davy, who wanted to change the subject.

"Great fun, I assure you! We have dance parties every night."

"And do you dance?" said Davy.

"Dance?" said the Whale, with a reverberating chuckle. I'm as nimble as a sixpence. With these words the Whale shot through the air like a flying elephant and disappeared with a great splash in the sea.

Davy stood watching the spot where he went down,

but he soon discovered that the Whale had gone for good. Feeling quite lonesome, he sat down on the sand and gazed mournfully out upon the sea.

The wind began to blow fiercely. Presently the air was filled with lobsters, eels, and wriggling fishes that were being carried inshore by the wind. Suddenly a dog came sailing along. He was being helplessly blown about among the lobsters, uneasily jerking his tail from side to side to keep it out of reach of their great claws. Davy caught him by the ear as he was going by and landed him in safety on the beach. He proved to be a very shaggy animal. It had an old pea-jacket, with a weather-beaten hat jammed on the side of his head, and a patch over one eye.

"Are you a pointer?" he said at last, by way of opening conversation.

"Not I," said the Dog, sulkily. "It's rude to point. I'm an old Sea-Dog, come ashore in a gale. What's *your* name?"

"Davy —" began the little boy, but before he could say another word the old Sea-Dog growled, "Right you are!" And with this the old Sea-Dog began to walk around and around in circles reciting a poem to Davy, whom he mistook for Davy Jones. Just at this moment the old Sea-Dog, who had been constantly increasing his speed, disappeared in a most extraordinary manner in a whorling cloud of sand. Davy, who was also spinning, discovered that he himself was rapidly boring his way, down into the beach. Before he could make an effort to free himself, he felt himself going down through the beach, with the sand pouring in upon him as if he had been inside of a huge hourglass. He landed with a gentle thump, flat on his back, with tall grass waving about him.

When Davy sat up and looked around he found himself in a beautiful meadow. At a little distance the Goblin was sitting on the grass. He was examining a great, struggling creature that he was holding down by its wings.

"What is it?" asked Davy.

"It's a Cricket-Bat," said the Goblin. "His body is like a bat and his wings are like a pair of umbrellas." He tossed the great creature over to Davy and walked away.

The Cricket-Bat made a swoop at Davy and then flew away across the meadow. It dashed here and there at flying things. Turning on its side, it knocked them quite out of sight. To Davy's delight, the Cockalorum came into view, flying across the meadow. At the sight of him the Cricket-Bat ran at the great creature and knocked him down into the tall grass.

Davy ran to the spot where the Cockalorum had fallen and found him sitting helplessly in the grass.

"I didn't do it," cried Davy, trying to keep from laughing. "It was the Cricket-Bat. He was only having a game of cricket with you."

The Cockalorum pondered over this for a moment and then said, "I prefer croquet."

"Laughing always gives me a stomach-ache," said the Goblin. "There's a buttercup behind you. Could you please get me some water."

For a moment, Davy felt very strange. He felt as though his head and arms and legs were all trying to get inside of his jacket.

Davy picked the buttercup and hurried away across the meadow. Presently he came upon a sparkling little spring, gently bubbling. He was just bending over to dip

the buttercup into the spring, when the ground under his feet began to shake and he was thrown into the water.

Davy came sputtering to the top of the water and scrambled ashore. To his astonishment he saw that the spring had spread itself out into a little lake. The grass had grown to an enormous height. Then he was startled by a tremendous roar of laughter. Looking around, he saw the Goblin, now seeming at least twenty feet high, standing beside the spring. The Goblin was laughing with all of his might. "Another minute and you would have been no bigger than a peanut!"

"What's the matter with me?" cried Davy.

"Why, you fell into an elastic spring," laughed the Goblin.

"I don't think that there's anything to laugh about," said Davy. "What am I going to do?"

"Oh! don't worry," said the Goblin. "I'll take a dip myself, just to be friendly, and tomorrow morning we can get back to any size you like."

He jumped into the spring, and a moment later climbed out exactly Davy's size.

"Now what do you say to a ride on a field-mouse?"

"That will be wonderful!" said Davy.

"It will be evening soon," said the Goblin, "and moonlight is the time for mouse-back riding."

The Goblin took Davy by the hand and led him through the wood. "Freckles," he called, "what time is it?"

"Forty-croaks," answered a toad, who was resting on a lily pad. Then in the pool, he heard another toad croak. "That makes it forty-one croaks," said the toad. "The snoopers have come in, and Thimbletoes is shaking in his

boots." The toad hopped away.

"What does that mean?" asked Davy.

"It means that the fairies are in and we don't get our ride," said the Goblin glumly. "You see, Thimbletoes is the Prime Minister for the Queen of the Fairies. If one of the snoopers finds out something that the Queen doesn't know, then the Prime Minister loses his job and the snooper takes it."

They came to a little building about the size of a doll house. It was lit by a vast number of fireflies. They hung from the ceiling by loops of cobwebs. The field- mice were kept in little stalls. To Davy's amazement, the far side of the building was filled with fairies. They had shining clothes and gauzy wings sparkling in the soft light. Just beyond them Davy saw the Queen sitting on a raised throne, and beside her was the Prime Minister, who looked upset.

"Now here's this Bandybug," said the Prime Minister, "to think he has the nerve to tell you that he can hear the bark of a dogwood tree or untie the knots in a cord of wood!"

"Bosh!" cried the Queen. "Paint him with raspberry jam, and put him to bed in a beehive. Bring in Berrylegs."

Berrylegs, who proved to be a wiry little Fairy, was immediately brought in. His little wings stood up sharply. His manner, was so fresh, that Davy felt certain there was going to be trouble.

"May it please your highness," said Berrylegs, "I've found out how the needles get into the haystacks."

"Oh, come now," said the Prime Minister. "That's not fair, you know." No one paid attention to him.

As Berrylegs said this, a terrible lot of noise arose at once among the fairies.

Berrylegs, who was now swelling with importance called out, in a loud voice, "It comes from using sewing machines when they sow the hay-seed."

The Prime Minister gave a cry, and fell flat on his face. The Queen began jumping up and down. Suddenly a large Cat walked into the stable. The fairies fled in all directions. There was no mistaking the Cat, and Davy exclaimed, "Why! it's Solomon!"

The next instant the lights went out. Davy found himself in total darkness, with Solomon's eyes shining at him like two balls of fire.

There was a sound of sobs and cries and the squeaking of mice, among which could be heard the Goblin's voice crying, "Davy! Davy!" Then the stable was lifted off the ground and shaken very hard.

"That's Solomon, trying to get at the mice," thought Davy. "I wish that the old thing had stayed away," he said aloud. Just then the building broke into bits. Davy found himself sitting on the ground on the forest.

The moon had disappeared, and snow was falling. The sound of distant bells reminded Davy that Christmas day had come.

Solomon's eyes were shining in the darkness like a pair of lamps. As Davy sat looking at them, a light began to glow between them. The Goblin appeared, dressed in red, as when he first had come. As Davy gazed at him, he grew brighter and finally burst into a blaze. Then Solomon's eyes gradually took the form of great brass balls.

The reddish light was shining through his stomach again, as though the coals had been fanned back into life. Davy looked at the Goblin who was blazing with flame.

As the light of the fire grew brighter the trees around him slowly took the shape of an old-fashioned fireplace. Davy found himself curled up in the big easychair. His dear old grandmother was bending over him and saying gently, "Davy! Davy! Come and have some dinner, my dear!"

The Believing Voyage was ended.

ABOUT THE ILLUSTRATOR

Greg Hildebrandt was born in Detroit, Michigan in 1939. As a child, Greg and his twin brother, Tim, loved to read. Even more, they loved pictures. They spent hours looking at the works of many famous artists. As they grew up, the twins learned how to draw and paint. They moved to New Jersey and began to paint children's books. In 1976, they won a gold medal for being the best illustrators in America. Later, they painted the world - famous poster for the first "Star Wars" movie.

In 1983, Greg began illustrating the classics. He uses real people to pose for each character. Many of his models are his friends and family. Some of the books he has illustrated are *Peter Pan, Pinocchio, and The Wizard of Oz.*